RUFUS *and His* ANGRY TAIL

By Elias Carr
Illustrated by Michael Garton

Book design: Tim Palin Creative

Library of Congress Cataloging-in-Publication Data

Names: Carr, Elias, author. | Garton, Michael, illustrator.
Title: Rufus and his angry tail / by Elias Carr ; illustrated by Michael Garton.
Description: Minneapolis : Sparkhouse Family, [2016]. | Summary: Rufus the dog gets angry when his friend, Ava the lamb, bothers him while he is trying to play his horn.
Identifiers: LCCN 2015046598 | ISBN 9781506410494 (hardcover : alk. paper)
Subjects: | CYAC: Anger--Fiction. | Dogs--Fiction. | Sheep--Fiction. | Christian life--Fiction.
Classification: LCC PZ7.C229323 Ruf 2016 | DDC [E]--dc23 LC record available at http://lccn.loc.gov/2015046598

The paper used in this publication meets the minimum requirements of the American National Standard for Information Sciences—Permanence of Paper for Printed Library Materials, ANSI Z329.48-1984.

Printed in the United States of America

24 23 22 21 20 19 18 17 16 1 2 3 4 5 6 7 8 9 10

VN0004589; 9781506410494; MAY2016

This is Rufus, and this is his horn.

Whenever Rufus played his horn,
his tail wagged.

When he couldn't find his horn, Rufus's tail drooped. But one day, Rufus's tail did something different.

Something angry!

Rufus was standing on the big rock and playing his horn. His tail was wagging happily when Ava came along with a bucket full of mud.

Ava set down the bucket. "Hey, Rufus!" she called. "Can I use your horn to stir this mud?"

Rufus's tail began to bristle. His horn was for playing, not stirring. He didn't want his horn all muddy!

So Ava stirred the mud with her hoof.
She began to make mud pies.
"She's making a terrible mess," Rufus grumbled to himself. "She'd better stop."

But Ava didn't stop. And now her mud pies needed squishing. What a mess!

Rufus's tail bristled and twisted. He decided to play his horn somewhere else.

Rufus found a log by the stream where he could play his horn. He tooted his horn up and played a song for the clouds.

He tooted his horn down and played a song for the rocks. He sounded amazing!

But now Ava's mud pies were ready . . .
and she wanted to sell them right
where Rufus was playing his horn.

“Pies for sale!” Ava called.
“Fresh mud pies, extra squishy!
Come and get them!”

Rufus's tail bristled and twisted and prickled. He'd had enough of Ava and her mud pies. He blew his horn right in Ava's face.

Ava tumbled to the ground.

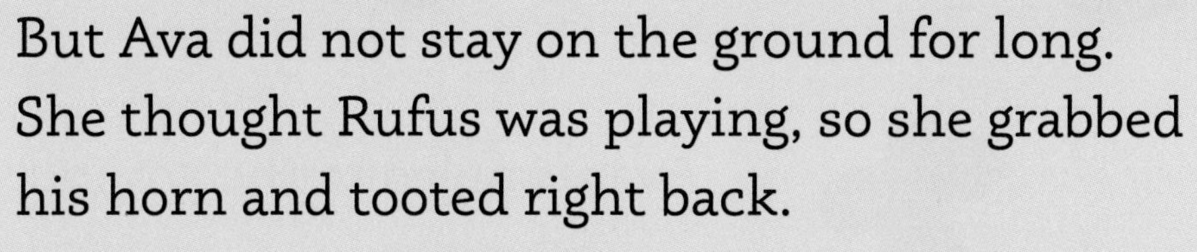

But Ava did not stay on the ground for long. She thought Rufus was playing, so she grabbed his horn and tooted right back.

Rufus was so surprised that he stumbled and fell right into the stream.

Rufus's tail bristled and twisted and prickled and shook. His fur felt hot. His insides felt tingly. He was so angry with Ava!

"Stop! I don't like that!" he yelled. Ava stopped.

"You took my horn! You got mud on me! And now I'm ALL WET!" bellowed Rufus.

Ava’s tail curled under.

"I thought you wanted to play," Ava said.
"I'm sorry I made you so mad, Rufus."

Rufus didn't know what to say. He dove underwater to wash the mud from his fur. Ava had said she was sorry. Rufus's tail relaxed.

Dear God,

I'm tired of feeling angry.
Help me not be so angry anymore
so that I can feel more peaceful.

Amen.

Rufus popped back up. “I forgive you, Ava,” he said. “I know you didn’t mean to make me angry.”

“Will you play with me?” Ava asked hopefully.

Rufus’s tail began to wag.

“Yes,” he said. “But first you need a bath too!”

ABOUT THE STORY

Rufus and Ava get along. . .until they don't. A prayer to feel calmer helps Rufus reset and deal with feeling mad.

DELIGHT IN READING TOGETHER

When you read this story, your voice and facial expressions can show the increasing anger that Rufus feels.

ABOUT YOUNG CHILDREN AND NEW FRIENDS

Anger is one of the first emotions we experience in our lives. Long before we can name this feeling, we show anger in our faces, voices, and bodies. As a caregiver, you can help young children learn to recognize anger, name it, and manage it.

A FAITH TOUCH

God created us to experience feelings—all of the feelings! We may feel angry when things don't go our way. We are loved by a God who is loving, merciful, and slow to anger.

The Lord is gracious and merciful, slow to anger and abounding in steadfast love.

Psalm 145:8

SAY A PRAYER

Share this prayer Rufus said when he felt angry:

Dear God, I'm tired of being angry. Help me not feel so angry anymore so that I can feel more peaceful.

Amen.